Caroline S. Henton

Little Creatures

Olympia Publishers
London

www.olympiapublishers.com
OLYMPIA PAPERBACK EDITION

A CIP catalogue record for this title is
available from the British Library.

ISBN: 978-1-78830-427-6

This is a work of fiction.
Names, characters, places and incidents originate from the writer's
imagination. Any resemblance to actual persons, living or dead, is
purely coincidental.

First Published in 2019

Olympia Publishers
60 Cannon Street
London
EC4N 6NP
Printed in Great Britain

Dedication

This book is dedicated to my dear daughters: Victoria Louise, Alexandra Rachel and Harriet Rose.

Acknowledgement

I wish to express my thanks and gratitude to Jordan Weeks, for all his support, and his dedication and passion for this period in our history expressed through his assistance in bringing the little creatures to life in the early stages of their characterisation.

Foreword

World War One was a deadly conflict killing over 16 million people, and causing around 37 million civilian and military casualties. Families were torn apart, losing fathers, brothers, husbands and sons and those men who did return would never be the same again. Unable to talk about the horrors that they had experienced and endured, these brave men took to their graves stories of heroic acts and deeds, of which sadly we will never know.

Little Creatures acknowledges and honours these unsung heroes, through gentle and creative symbolisation in a way that younger readers can understand and relate to. It also teaches them to believe in themselves, use their skills and talents and the power of what can be achieved when we lay aside our differences and work together.

Like the fictional characters in the story, the sacrifice and commitment of the Merchant Navy in conflict has often been overlooked and unacknowledged. I am therefore delighted that the author has chosen to donate 10p for every book sold to the Merchant Navy Association who work tirelessly to raise awareness and recognition of the war time contributions of our seafarers.

"As the autumn leaves begin to fall, we will think about our unsung heroes and remember them all."

Bruno Peek
Bruno Peek LVO OBE OPR
Pageantmaster
Battle's Over - A Nation's Tribute

Preface

In the evenings as dusk fell, a big toad would come and sit outside our porch at our country home in rural Normandy, France. The children decided it was as if he was on sentry duty. The house was occupied by the Nazis during the Second World War, as the previous owner had discovered, when he decided to renovate the property and had uncovered the blue paint on the walls, the Nazi sign of occupation.

Looking at the toad each evening, sitting firmly to attention, it got me thinking... and the idea of the story of Lily the Ladybird and her fellow little creatures and their combined war effort to save a French village from foreign occupation began!

Introduction

In London's Park Lane you will find a war memorial inscribed 'Animals in War'.

This monument is dedicated to 'all the animals that served and died alongside British and Allied forces in wars and campaigns throughout time. They had no choice'.

This story is dedicated to all the unsung heroes in the Great War, whose stories will never be known. From man to beast, to the tiniest creatures on the earth who all contributed in their own ways.

Thank you
Merci

Prologue

Bobby Bee buzzed back to the hive. He flew slowly and felt sad. Queen Bee smiled at him. "What is the matter, Bobby Bee?" she asked. I thought you would be happy flying around, happy and free?"

"But I am so small," said Bobby, "compared to the other animals I see; the dogs and cats, the foxes and rabbits, the pigeons and the horses. What use am I?"

"Listen," said Queen Bee, "stop your buzzing, and I will tell you a story from the Great War; a story that will teach you how all creatures on earth have their strengths, no matter how big or small they are, and how even the smallest creatures can achieve great things… listen Bobby Bee…"

And so the story began…

The Boche

Lily was alone, Lily was shaking, Lily was scared. She could hear the thud, thud, thud of the soldiers' feet. Thud, thud, thud, the Boche troops were advancing. She cowered in the crevice of a tree stump. Thud, thud, thud. As the soldiers marched by, Lily looked at their faces. Serious faces, with cold, hard eyes. These soldiers clearly meant business and they were marching towards the village. What could Lily the ladybird do?

She thought deeply, as ladybirds do, and decided a 'Little Creatures' meeting needed to be called at once. Resistance was needed urgently in order to save the village of Mariot. Lily had heard what had happened in the neighbouring village of Herve. The Boche soldiers had taken all the villagers' food and they had moved into their houses. Villagers had ended up sleeping in the barns, cold and hungry with their animals. When the Boche had moved on, they had taken the men of the village away as prisoners, and had set fire to the villagers' homes. Herve had been destroyed! The village was no more.

Lily the ladybird was alone, Lily was shaking, Lily was scared, but Lily had to do something, and she had to do something quickly. She knew it was just a matter of days before the soldiers reached Mariot.

The Little Creatures had saved the town of Ramet; they had organised themselves well and stopped the Boche from advancing. Unfortunately, in Herve, some of the creatures hadn't believed the reality of what was happening in the country. They thought the Boche would just stop for something to eat, and if the people were nice to them, the Boche would be nice back, and then move on, grateful for a taste of French hospitality and a chance to indulge in some *joie de vivre*. By the time the creatures of the village had realised that these soldiers did not think, act or feel the same, that they were in fact killing machines, it was too, too late. Lily sat for a moment and thought about the family of the garden she used to fly over from time to time. She thought about the laughter she used to hear, watching the family sitting out drinking fine wines, eating their cheeses and fresh baguettes, and chatting about their day, the children shrieking with delight as they caught fish in the little stream that ran along the bottom of the garden. The sound of the cicadas chatting happily and the birds singing and enjoying flying up above. The family tended their vegetables and shared their produce proudly with their neighbours. There were always plenty of aphids for Lily to eat. Now it was silent and Lily realised she hadn't heard the birds singing for a long time. Her beloved homeland was changing. The father had been killed by the Boche as he tried to protect his home. The Boche had moved into the house and painted it blue, a sign of Boche occupation. Lily didn't like the colour blue. The mother and the children had fled. No one knew where. There were stories that some families were living in the forest. Lily had not seen or heard them, but she guessed they were having to be very careful so as not to reveal where they were. Were they even still alive?

Lily became angry; her beloved country was being destroyed piece by piece. She became even more determined. I may be small and people may think I have no voice, she thought, but my heart and my head are strong. Claude the grasshopper had always told her that, a strong heart and a strong head are all you need, Lily, and the wisdom to know how to use them. Claude was very wise. "I shall use them," she whispered out loud to herself, "I shall use them and… and I think I know how…"

It was dusk now, the sun was beginning to set. Lily flew off towards the pond. Lily was little, Lily had small wings, and it was a long way, but she knew how important it was that she got to the pond. Every now and then she stopped for a little rest, but not for too long because she knew she could so easily give up; just a little rest here and a little rest there, just enough, just enough, to get to the pond. Lily had to find Antoine and the ant colony that had recently moved to the rocks nearby. As she got there she could see them all scurrying around. Busy, busy, busy, always busy, she thought to herself, do they never get weary?

She spotted Antoine. There he was directing some of the younger ants. Antoine had moved here from Herve. Antoine had seen many things; although he didn't talk about it, Lily knew this. Lily knew Antoine was wise, and Antoine had a strong heart and a strong head; perhaps sadly a heart that had been broken by sadness and despair and a head that had seen confusion and panic, but a heart and a head that had survived, when so many hadn't. Antoine had strong eyes too, eyes that had perhaps seen too much. But vision was going to be important; Lily knew she needed Antoine's vision. This had been the reason for the recent success of the resistance efforts of the Little Creatures in Ramet. Antoine's vision and all creatures working together as a team, giving their strengths, with their hearts and their heads, using their eyes, their ears, their feet, and if it needed it, their souls. This was the only way to defeat cold killing machines. Lily knew this. Evil cannot fight a soul. Evil does not understand a soul. As Lily flew towards the pond, she knew now she was prepared to use her soul, and with Antoine's vision, there would be a plan.

"*Bonsoir*, Antoine. Good evening," called Lily.

"Ah, *bonsoir, ma petite coccinelle, ca va?*" replied Antoine. "My lady beetle is looking as beautiful as ever!"

"*Merci*, Antoine, thank you," said Lily, "but I am here on serious business. I bring news. It's not good, it's not good. The Boche are heading towards Mariot. I saw their faces, Antoine. Cold serious faces. Cold, hard eyes. I could not see any love. I could not see any care for us or our beloved France. They look like the killing machines that destroyed Herve."

For a second Antoine said nothing; he stared into the distance as if he was reliving what had happened to his home and the people there. Then he turned to Lily, and said, "Well done for bringing this news, Lily. I shall call a Little Creatures meeting at once. We need to plan."

The Song of the Cicadas - le Chant des Cigales.

The humming was quiet at first; Lily could barely hear it as she sat next to Antoine on the rock. "Listen, Lily," he said, "it will get louder…"

And it did. Louder and louder till the sound filled the forest. "The cicadas are sending out a distress call," explained Antoine. "The creatures will be here soon."

"Won't it alert the Boche?" asked Lily.

"No," said Antoine, "that is one of the cicadas' strengths. The sound they are making today is too high pitched to be heard by humans."

As the sound continued, small creatures began to arrive and congregate by the pond. The ants all stood still and to attention as commanded by Antoine. Antoine was a fine commander and everyone respected him. Antoine had seen things. Antoine knew things. Antoine was wise. The frogs and toads jumped off the lily pads and came and sat on the rocks. There were snails and spiders, wasps and bees. There were even bats, though the sun still hadn't quite set.

The creatures came from all over the forest and sat there quietly while Lily explained what she had seen. Lily had a small voice but her heart and her head made her voice seem loud to all those who listened. She spoke clearly and told them about the soldiers' faces and the soldiers' eyes. Antoine would not talk about what had happened in Herve but he explained that Lily was right to be fearful and that now a plan of action was needed. He gave a speech.

"I want you all to think about your strengths," he said "We have all been given strengths that, combined, will make a powerful army which can defeat the killing machines which have invaded our land. If you have a strong heart, a strong head and use the strengths which have been given to you all, we can save Mariot. Think deeply, little creatures, what are your strengths...?"

Lily sat and thought about hers. "People think I am pretty and I have no voice," she said.

"But I see things, I feel things, I think deeply. I am full of care and my heart and my head make my voice seem loud to those who listen. I can fly; I can fly higher and faster and for longer than even humans realise, and I can exude my yellow poison if I have to fight with my soul. I love the people in Mariot, the gardens, the forest, our lives and our liberty and I shall use my soul..."

The snails sat and thought, the spiders sat and thought, the frogs and toads sat and thought, the wasps and bees sat and thought, and the bats and the ants too. Antoine sat and thought deeply. Antoine sat and thought hard. Antoine thought of a plan.

Termites

Theon was sitting on a rock in the middle of the red-hot dusty path, basking in the midday sun, when he heard the cicadas.

Cicadas at noon? Theon thought. Why are they not singing their song at dusk? But this was not a song, this was a message. Theon listened. He listened hard. This message was serious. This message was sad and it was urgent.

Theon left the path and went to find the other termites. "We have to leave here. We have to travel north at once," he said.

"But Father" said Little Thierry, "we belong in the south. No termites from here have ever travelled north."

"You are right, my son," said Theon. "We have lived here for tens of thousands of years since the dinosaurs but if we are to continue enjoying our home here, then we must save the homes of others or France will be destroyed. Our fellow creatures in the north need our help, they need our strengths. It will be a long journey, it will be a difficult journey but we shall move as a colony and work together as we have always done. I want to grow old hearing the cicadas singing their songs, not passing messages of sadness and sorrow. Antoine has sent for us."

"Antoine? Antoine the ant?" said the termites in unison. "An ant has sent for us and you want us to go? Are you crazy? We don't want to be ant breakfast, ant dinner, ant tea, or even ant supper! Ants and termites don't get on; ants and termites are enemies, ever since the time of the dinosaurs!"

"I understand your worries," reassured Theon. "However, when our country is in danger, it is well known that all little creatures work together. It has worked well in the village of Remet. Antoine has promised that no ant will be eating any of us for breakfast, lunch, tea or even supper! We will leave at dusk."

Theon turned to his son. "As we march, think of your strengths, Thierry. You are one of the most observant termites we have. You will see things; you will be our eyes on the journey that lies ahead."

"*Oui*, Papa, yes Papa, I will think of my strengths," replied Thierry, looking around.

As Theon ordered, the colony left their home in the sun at dusk. As thousands of termite soldiers made their way along the coast, Theon again heard the cicadas. "Bon chance; good luck, dear friends," they clicked and hummed in chorus from the trees.

"*Merci, merci beaucoup*, thank you very much," replied the termites.

Thierry followed tightly behind his father. "Stay on alert, Thierry," said his father.

"Father," replied Thierry, "we termites are always on high alert; it is what we do. You have taught me that."

"You have learnt your lesson well, my son," said Theon, smiling.

The cicadas hummed and clicked louder and more urgently. It was another message.

A message from Antoine.

Theon listened and then said to the termite troops, "We will eat as we go, as is our way, but we will be targeting the Boche camps. This is part of Antoine's plan. The Boche are stealing the food from France, so we must take from them. We must weaken these killing machines to save Mariot and all the other villages. Without the villages, there is no France."

As they went on their way, Thierry muttered to himself as all termites do, "I'm hungry now, I'm hungry now," and he started to look out for signs and evidence of Boche camps.

Night fell but the termites kept moving through the villages looking for signs of the Boche.

Then Thierry spotted a light in the distance. The light was moving; it was a lantern swinging backwards and forwards in the gentle breeze. As the termites grew closer, they could see a group of about fifty men. They look so young, thought Little Thierry. Are they really the Boche? But it was true; it was a Boche camp. The men were sitting and chatting together on the grass, and as Thierry got closer, he could see the hardness in their faces and the coldness in their eyes. Killing machines with no souls, thought Thierry. The men had set up their camp next to a neighbouring farm and were enjoying the produce they had stolen from the farmer.

"Look, Father," said Thierry, "what shall we do?"

Theon spotted what seemed to be some kind of trench.

"We wait here until the Boche go to sleep," he ordered the troops and they marched down into the long narrow ditch. It was muddy and smelt of human faeces and urine and it soon became clear that rats had claimed it as their home. The rats were the biggest Thierry had ever seen; as big as cats.

They seemed surprised when they saw the termites but ignored them and carried on with their rat business, as all rats generally do.

It wasn't long before, one by one, the Boche began to slumber, their bellies full, with their rifles by their sides. Little Thierry noticed that there were tiny creatures crawling all over them, and many of the Boche were covered in red bites. He asked them what they were doing. Lara, one of the lice nearest to Thierry turned to him and replied quietly, "We had news from the north from Antoine. The cicadas told us we needed to use our strengths to help defeat the Boche, to save our lives and our land. So we bite these men with their cold hard eyes and are giving them trench fever."

"What is that?" asked Thierry.

"It gives them headaches, fever and muscle pain," replied Lara, "and they are unable to fight. The best time to get them is when they are asleep. Some of them are even ending up with typhus and are dying. They try to get rid of us, but we can produce up to a dozen fresh eggs every day. The hospitals are starting to fill up with Boche casualties."

"*Merci, merci*, Lara," said Theon who had joined his son. "Antoine will be pleased. His plan is coming together." He then turned to his colony of termites and ordered them to leave the trench, infiltrate the camp and eat everything in sight! By the time they had finished, there was absolutely nothing left for the Boche when they awakened for breakfast.

"Well done, troops," said Theon. "Antoine will be pleased. Now we move on…"

And so they did, stopping at every Boche camp they found, waiting till the soldiers were asleep then quietly infiltrating the camps, devouring all the Boche's food supplies. They used the light kindly provided by the glow-worms to see their way. "We had news from the north from Antoine. The cicadas told us we needed to use our strengths to help defeat the Boche, to save our lives and our land," they said. "We are many and the French army are now putting us in our thousands in jars to use us as torches and lanterns so that they may read the maps when the sun goes down."

"*Merci, merci*, thank you, thank you," whispered the termites, "for your light."

"*Merci, merci*," replied the glow-worms, "for your appetites. Without their rations, the killing machines that have invaded our beloved homeland will weaken."

The terrain became unfamiliar and the termites reached a crossroads that Theon had never seen before.

"Which way? Which way?" the termites asked impatiently. They wanted to eat again, and it had been a while since they had seen a Boche camp.

"Look, Father," said Thierry, and he pointed to a silvery track on the road going straight ahead.

"Snail slime," said his father. "Another part of Antoine's plan! Well done, little Thierry. We follow the slime!"

So they did; the silvery tracks glistened in the sunshine, guiding them north. Every now and then the termites glanced at the l'escargots, sheltering in their shells from the hot afternoon sun. When Thierry looked back, Sebastien, the head of the snails, crawled out and wriggled around, as if to wish him luck.

"We had news from the north, from Antoine," called Sebastien. "The cicadas told us to use our strengths, to save our lives and to save our land."

"*Merci, merci*, thank you," called back Thierry, as he and the termite troop soldiered on. As they travelled further north, they could hear the booms and roar of shell fire. The air became dark from the smoke. Thierry felt scared and apprehensive. What was this world they were now entering? How was this France, the beloved homeland? It was a battle. Thierry saw wounded men and young boys being stretchered to dressing stations, some delirious and crying out with pain. "*Maman, Maman*," some of them cried. "Save me." The screams; Thierry thought he would never forget the sound of the screams and the desperation in the faces of those men. Some didn't seem old enough to be away from their

mothers. It was madness. He looked further ahead and could see the battlefield, and the devastation. The trees stood branchless and leafless, blown apart by the explosions. There was nothing but mud, mud, mud. Not the hard, red, baked soil of the south; thick, wet, brown, oozing mud, that the afternoon sunshine had been unable to dry out. "This area has had the worse rainfall in thirty years," explained Theon to his son.

Thierry saw soldiers knee deep in it, struggling and sinking. There was wire, wire everywhere, and then Thierry noticed the horses. He had never seen so many horses. Not the beautiful creatures he knew them for, but tired horses, lying in the mud, or caught up in the wires with broken limbs and broken souls. Now Thierry understood; man had always been able to deal with their own affairs, but this war was affecting the creatures of their land. The big ones were struggling; it was important that all the little creatures played their part.

Theon called the termite march to a halt.

"Termites," he said, "look around you. This is why we have travelled so far from the south. These scenes will be remembered for generations to come and you will be remembered as the termites who helped to save France. We must do all we can to stop the savagery and devastation that we see around us. We must be brave and use our strengths to stop the Boche advancing any further. Termites, do not panic. Never since the time of the dinosaurs, has a termite ever panicked. We deal with things in an orderly fashion, following our rules. I remind you that we are a superorganism that for the last

300 million years have sacrificed our own personal well-being for the good of everyone. That is indeed our strength, that and our numbers. Our colonies are many, and when we are done, other colonies will advance also. Together we outnumber the Boche many, many times. We are expected in the meadows around Mariot this evening. We are worker termites who eat wood and build tunnels. That is what we do, and Antoine needs us with all our strengths for his plan. Now rest awhile. Termites don't sleep, unlike those ants, we don't need sleep, but we do need to rest, for there will be much to do later…"

Theon, Thierry and the termite troops stopped and rested, watching in horror at the scenes that unfolded before them. This was war, a war that was being waged on their soil, the soil that meant so much to them; the soil that termites engineered into their mounds and homes, the soil that provided the food that nourished the soul of their beloved France. They saw men with rifles leaping out of trenches and running towards the Boche, screams, cries, the sound of gunfire, shells and mortars. Men falling to the ground, men leaning on each other, helping each other to find their way back to the trenches. There was the sound of scampering rats; the rats they had seen before. Thierry wondered what strengths the rats had. Could they not help? But the rats carried on with their rat business as rats generally do. The air was heavy and noisy. The feeling and sounds of suffering were all around and impossible to escape.

I must use my strengths to stop the Boche, thought Thierry as he looked around.

As the termites continued their journey, Thierry looked back. One of the trees, broken and blackened from battle, caught his eye for on the trunk was a bright orange butterfly.

Thierry looked back again to check that he was not seeing things. There it was. Not just an orange butterfly, a bright beautiful butterfly, which glistened and shone despite the air being dark and thick with the smoke from guns and shell fire. "Papillon, Papillon," little Thierry called. But no one heard him; the rest of the troop were focussed on marching to Mariot. Little Thierry felt a strange sense of hope and happiness inside. It is a sign, he thought. To see Papillon is a sign.

"*Merci, mon cherie,*" he called, "*merci...*" He was sure that Papillon fluttered her wings in reply. When he looked around again, she was gone.

The Arrival – L'arrivee

Lily spied a tree stump near the creek at Bogues Wood. That will do, that will do, she thought. Lily was tired and needed to rest. She had been flying backwards and forwards, backwards and forwards all day long checking how far the Boche had advanced to Mariot and reporting back to Antoine. Frederick the bullfrog had organised the frogs and toads to do the same on the ground, using their 360 degree vision and their loud calls. Claude and the other grasshoppers had been listening carefully and picking up the vibrations of the Boche movements with their legs. Lily only had a quiet voice, but she had her wings and her spirit and she was determined to use it. Fortunately, the Boche had stopped at a farm outside the village, and seemed to be setting up camp for the night. So Lily nibbled on a few aphids and rested on the stump for a while, recharging her weakened body. It was weak, but her spirit remained strong. I have a strong head and a strong heart and I care. I will use my soul if I need to, she reminded herself, that will be enough to help defeat the men with the cold hard eyes. After a few minutes, she returned to the pond.

Not long after, the creatures at the pond heard the sound of marching. "It's the termites! They have arrived!" shouted Antoine. And what a sight they were to behold as they entered the clearing around the pond. "Left right, left right," ordered Theon. "Termite troops… halt!" And as tired and weary as they were, the termites proudly stood to attention in front of Antoine.

Antoine commanded the ants to fall in behind them. Thierry whispered to his fellow ant, Tobias, "Who would have thought, us and ants, us and ants…!"

Antoine welcomed the termites to Bogues Wood. He explained how all little creatures needed to use their strengths to save their homeland. The spiders called out, "We already are, Antoine. We thought about what you said and we have been providing our strong silky webs to the French soldiers to make the crosshairs in their gunsights."

"Excellent, spiders," praised Antoine. Then he told all the creatures to relax while he and Theon went and sat on a rock and discussed the latest events in France. Thierry and Tobias went to talk to Lily. "Who would have thought," they said in chorus, "ants and termites, ants and termites."

"And spiders and grasshoppers too," said Lily. "Remember this always," said Lily. "Remember how we came together and tell your story to all who will hear. History has a way of hiding true heroes, and little creatures are invisible to many. Man does what man does and only a few ever notice the world beneath their feet. They use their brains but not always their vision. My body is weak, although my spirit is strong. I am using my strengths but I do not know if I will be able to tell my story."

"Lily, I know everything is going to be OK," said little Thierry.

"How do you know, how can you be so sure?" asked Lily.

"Because I saw Papillon. In a battlefield on a blackened tree, I saw Papillon. The spirit of France will resist and return, Lily."

"I hope you are right, little Thierry. Let us rest awhile."

The Plan: Le Plan

The cicadas sang: "Antoine's plan, Antoine's plan," and the little creatures gradually gathered once more round the pond in Bogues Wood. Antoine stood up on a rock and held up a big log, three times his size. The little creatures gasped. "Look," he said, "we are strong, little creatures are strong. Ants can carry up to 50 times their own body weight. You all have your own strengths, and together we will use them to save our lives and our land.

"France is the homeland of the free. France is the land that feeds you and me. Together we work for victory." Antoine's eyes looked determined as he ordered the little creatures, "Repeat back to me…"

The creatures repeated proudly:

"France is the homeland of the free. France is the land that feeds you and me. Together we work for victory."

"The Boche are getting weaker," explained Antoine. "The termites have been devouring their food as they have made their way through France. They are less in numbers, now. However, they have now advanced to the farm outside Mariot, and we must stop them before they go any further."

Antoine talked about the bridge that led to Mariot, and he talked about the strengths that all the creatures could use to defeat the Boche if they worked together.

41

"So…" he said firmly," …we all meet back here when the light fades tonight. There is much to be done!"

Lily looked into her heart and her soul. Was she scared? No, she was proud to be playing her part, and she cared. She was determined, determined to save Mariot and see the villagers enjoying their lives and the land once more, determined to save her beloved homeland. Little Thierry looked into his heart. Was he scared? No, he trusted his father, Theon, and he trusted Antoine. He could see it in his eyes, that Antoine had seen things and knew things. Antione was a fine commander. He wanted to learn from them both and hoped to grow up and be as fine as they were one day. He had also seen the sign of the butterfly. Papillon, Papillon… he murmured to himself. Tobias looked into his heart. Was he scared? A little perhaps, but he had his friends, and the termite colony were many in numbers. He had seen many bad things, but he was also young and it was an adventure coming up from the south. Claude the grasshopper looked into his heart. Was he scared? No, he was old and had had his summer. He would use his remaining strength to defeat the Boche. A strong heart and strong head are all you need, he reminded himself. Sebastien looked into this heart. He was scared but he saw it as his duty to save the land; and his duty he would do. There was nothing else to think about. Snails are not prone to emotion; you know where you are with a snail. Little Thierry glanced up and thought he saw Papillon flying in and out of the reeds by the pond. He looked again, but she was gone… The spirit of France will resist, he told his heart, and will be free once more.

I know it…

The Attack – L'attaque

The light began to fade and the creatures came together once more. What a sight it was to behold. Ladybirds, frogs, toads, spiders, bees, wasps, glow-worms, bats, snails, ants and termites. They all stood proudly on parade waiting for orders. Antoine once again climbed onto the rock to address them all.

"This is it, Little Creatures," he said. "Be brave. The spirit of France is within us all and will protect us. France is the homeland of the free. Together we will achieve victory."

"France is the homeland of the free. Together we will achieve victory," Thierry repeated to himself.

"Termites, follow me," ordered Theon. "We go to the bridge…"

"Goodbye, Lily," called out Thierry. "See you in Mariot."

"*Au revoir*, little Thierry," replied Lily. "Remember to tell your story…"

The Boche had set up camp and one by one fell asleep. When the embers of their campfire had died out, the glow-worms arrived and shed a gentle light for the spiders. The spiders started to spin, and spin and spin, the biggest most intricate webs that have ever been seen in France. They hung their webs amongst the trees that led to the bridge to Mariot. Lily flew backwards and forwards, backwards and forwards, reporting to Antoine.

The termites followed the snail trails that Sebastien and the other snails had left, and marched towards the bridge that led to Mariot. The termites gasped when they arrived and saw the beautiful village they were to save. They felt even more determined that the Boche were not going to invade and destroy another piece of their beloved France as they had done in Herve. Theon led them underneath the bridge and directed them to the parts of the framework and structures which he wished them to chew. Little Thierry chomped away like he had never done before. "Well done, Thierry," said his father. "Use your strengths." Lily flew over and reported back to Antoine.

Morning came and the Boche stirred. Lily flew back and alerted Antoine, and he ordered the bees, and ants and wasps to advance. Hundreds of little creatures marched forwards, and as soon as they entered the camp, they attacked. They bit and they stang with all their might, no leg or arm of any Boche avoided the onslaught. Some of the Boche reacted with their legs swelling, and some went into shock, couldn't breathe and collapsed. The air was full of ear-piercing cries and screams, as the Boche struggled to understand what was happening to them. Some of them began to run towards the river to find relief, but the frogs and toads appeared, hopping about in front of them. Trip, trip, trip. The Boche fell this way and that way, nursing cuts and wounds as well as the burning of the stings. Those that managed to continue started to make their way to the bridge, and soon found themselves being caught and tangled up in the webs while the spiders looked on.

"Antoine, Antoine," Lily said breathlessly, but excitedly, "the Boche are being injured and are falling away. The plan is working, the plan is working."

"Excellent," said Antoine. "Let Theon know to expect the last of the Boche shortly."

"*Oui, bien sur*, of course, commander," said Lily. She gave a salute and then flew up again, flying with all her strength. Just as she got there, she felt very weak, and it took all her strength to pass Antoine's message.

"Lily, you look exhausted," remarked Theon. "Perhaps you need a rest from the front line."

"Everyone needs a rest from the front line to recharge. Can the bats not pass the messages to Antoine?"

"Bats come out in the dusk; if they come out now, it will arouse suspicions. They have their place all over France at dusk when they can use their strong sense of hearing and use their echo system to determine how far away the Boche are, and how fast they are travelling. I have done what I needed to do," said Lily. "I have one last thing to do. *Au revoir*, Theon."

It was time to fight with her soul. She flew in the direction of the Boche and administered her yellow poison to the first soldier she saw, biting him hard in the face, underneath the cold hard uncaring eyes that had made her so determined to save Mariot. Theon watched, then he saw Lily fly off into the forest. Theon knew that that would be the last he would see of Lily.

"*Merci*, brave little *coccinelle*," he whispered. "*Merci*. You will live on in the hearts and minds of all the little creatures. France will always be grateful and the *coccinelle* will be loved forever." He sang quietly to himself for a moment.

Little ladybird
You sang our song
Now fly over the rainbow
Knowing your story will live on

Little ladybird
So brave and so strong
Thank you, thank you
You did no wrong.

Petite coccinelle
Tu as chante notre chanson
Maintenant vole au dessus de l'arc-en-ciel
Sachant que ton histoire perdurera
Petite coccinelle
Si brave et si forte
Merci, merci
Tu n'as fait aucun tort.

The Boche approached the bridge, and began to march across, swinging their rifles.

"Mariot is nearly ours," cried their commander to those that were left. "Tonight we will stay in the houses here and devour the food of the villagers. Then we will take them all

prisoner and destroy their homes. Another village will belong to us." Just as he said that, part of the bridge fell away into the river down below. "Careful, troops," he ordered, "move to one side." But as they did that, another plank, and another plank fell away, under the weight of the Boche army. The Boche began to fall into the deep water, being pulled under by the strong current. "Help, help," they cried, but they were now too far and few between to be able to help each other. The Boche were defeated.

The little creatures stood and watched and let out a big cheer. "Hurray, hurray," they cried.

"How do we get to Mariot though, Father?" asked little Thierry.

"Look over there, Thierry," directed Theon, and he pointed to the riverbank where the ants had turned themselves into rafts by linking their bodies together.

"All aboard!" they cried. "All aboard to Mariot!"

Thierry climbed on first, calling out for Lily to join him, but she was nowhere to be seen. Perhaps she had flown over to Mariot, he thought. Tobias joined him, then Claude, and Sebastien and Frederick.

"Father, join me," he called out to Theon

"I will stay here," he said "until you have all got across. See you there, my son, and well done! *Bravo!*"

The ant rafts floated towards Mariot, and broke up when they got to the riverbank on the other side.

"Thank you, *merci, merci*," the little creatures all cried, and then ran up the bank and looked at the village that they had all had saved.

Antoine was already there to welcome them. "Little creatures, we have worked together for victory and now France will be free. Victory is ours. The Boche cannot enter this village and it will stop them advancing any further. For all over France now, little creatures will be doing the same as you have done tonight. Tonight, we enjoy the land that is ours. Feast as much as you like and sleep."

"Antoine, have you seen Lily?" called out Thierry.

Theon came across to Thierry and whispered quietly to him, "Lily did what she had to do, Thierry. She used her strengths and she used her soul. She will live on in the hearts and souls of all the little creatures in the land. We have worked together for victory and France will now be free. Never forget her, Thierry."

"I won't Father" he said. "And I will tell the story, as she asked me to."

"Look, Father. Look Father," cried out Thierry. A beautiful orange butterfly fluttered past and looked down on them both. "Papillon, Papillon," he cried and he felt a warm deep glow inside, that seemed as warm as the orange of the butterfly's wings which glowed in the sunshine.

"Today is a good day, Father," he said. "We have our way of life and our land back."

As he said that, the birds began to sing once more, the church bells of Mariot began to ring and the villagers came out of their houses and danced and sang. The little creatures all smiled and cheered, their hearts and souls overflowing with happiness, proud of what they had achieved. "Hurray," they cried.

That evening, Antoine called all the creatures together once more.

"Know this, little creatures," he said. "In years to come, man will honour their heroes, and remember their fallen. They will remember the big animals that helped in winning the war. They will recognise the courage that the horses made in transporting their weapons and belongings, and in carrying them into battle; the messages that the pigeons passed; the dogs that helped to rescue and comfort the wounded. Sadly, little creatures, man's vision will not allow him to know or understand the quiet ones, the small ones, the little creatures of the land that have proved such a resistance to the enemy. They will not know about the heroes that we have amongst us. But we know, and we will tell our stories for generations to come, in the fields, in the meadows and in the forests. I now order you little creatures that each year, as the autumn leaves begin to fall, we will think about our heroes and remember them all."

Epilogue

"So, you see, Bobby Bee," said Queen Bee, "know that no matter how small you are, you have strengths to use in your life. And know that when creatures work together, their strength becomes even stronger. You and the other little creatures are part of the fabric of our beloved France. Your ancestors weaved this by all working together.

"A termite I met when I travelled down south told me this story, and it is now my turn to pass it onto you Bobby."

"Was it Thierry?" asked Bobby.

"Yes, he told me his name was Thierry, and his last words to me were 'don't forget Lily', replied Queen Bee. "Use your strengths, Bobby, and enjoy being happy and free. Never forget Lily for she cared for you and she cared for me and she wanted us all to be happy and free."

Bonne nuit.
Good night